FREAKY FREDDY

RIVER

PAGE PUBLISHING
Conneaut Lake, PA

First originally published by Page Publishing 2023

ISBN 979-8-88654-730-6 (pbk)
ISBN 979-8-88654-744-3 (digital)

Printed in the United States of America

I fuck with Freaky Freddy.

—Unknown

Don't read this book.

—Unknown

AUTHOR'S NOTE

Warning: Parental supervision is heavily recommended no matter how old you are… Freddy, Ahem! Freaky Freddy is off the chain. This book is nasty, gruesome, disturbing, a little bit humorous, unforgettable, and *smack nasty*! My intent is not really to corrupt your thinking or scar your thoughts for life, but I can guarantee that you will recommend this. Oh, and if this book makes me a lot of money, I will make a sequel to this story… Advance at your own risk.

Freddy is a fictional character.

*Lyon Lake Correctional Institution: Lock up
5:37 p.m. September 11, Freddy's birthday*

Lt. Hickenbottom was the lucky contestant chosen to distribute the inmate's mail in lockup this evening. Unfortunately Freddy Dawson was not prepared for his appearance this time around.

"Mr. Dawson, I have a letter for you."

"A letter? Man, I wanna know when the fuck you clowns are gonna let me outta here! To hell with that letter."

"I don't have that answer for you, Mr. Dawson. All I know is that you've been under investigation for a murder homicide down there on the lower yard. Have any more comments or concerns?"

"Yes," Freddy stated. "Where's my inmate representation? What's up with that!"

Lt. Hickenbottom rolled his eyes then smirked in a smartass manner. "This is South Carolina. There is no such thing as an inmate representation. Here's your letter. I got mail to pass out to the rest of the guys."

Lt. Hickenbottom slid the letter under the crack of the door and carried on.

"YOU'RE LUCKY I DIDN'T THROW PISS OR SHIT AT YOU THIS TIME!" Freddy screamed.

He looked at the envelope and the sender's address—Mom. Well, that's crazy. Freddy has not heard from his mother in years.

What possibly could she have to say? Freddy opened the letter to find a small, typed note.

> Dear My Son,
>
> Words cannot describe how sorry I am for not reaching out to you sooner. I have been undergoing so much emotional pain, and it's been hard for me to build up the courage to contact you. I looked you up on the SCDC website and saw that you were in lockup, so I called the prison to find out why. All they told me is that you were under investigation. So please, please, please write me back to let me know that you are safe. I love you, my son, and happy birthday! I miss you so much.
>
> Love,
> Mom

Freddy's face showed no emotion.

Usually Freddy would rip up the letter and flush it down the toilet. But this time, he did the unexpected. He filled out his only indigent state envelope with his mother's address on it and started writing. It did not take him long to get his point across. Freddy then read his note that he just wrote, smiled, and started stroking his dick. He looked at the note once more.

> Dear Shallow Stress Ball,
>
> You always want a motherfucker to feel bad for you. That game isn't going to work on me. I'll be honest with you though… If you were a dude, I would dress you up like a bitch and fuck the shit outta you!

Freddy sealed the letter inside of the envelope and caught Lt. Hickenbottom as he was about to leave.

"Put this letter with all of your outgoing mail, please, sir," Freddy pleaded. "It's very important that she gets it." Freddy slid the letter under the door.

The officer picked it up and left out of the building.

"I've been waiting a long time to get that off my chest," Freddy said to himself then climbed back into bed.

CHAPTER 1

Like normal, Freddy was looking out the window of his cell into the hallway. Not like there was anything better to do. Myles, the inmate run-around worker for lockup, hit the wing and approached Freddy's door in a strangely happy mood.

"What's up, Big Dog!" Myles said with enthusiasm.

Freddy really liked Myles because he was a very upstanding person, and he was one of the only people that looked out for him.

"Nothing much, dude. Why are you in such a good mood today?"

"I always try to stay in a good mood," Myles exclaimed with a smile. "In fact, I have some good news for you, Freddy!"

Freddy looked up at Myles. "All right, shoot!"

"Check this. I was standing by the control room door and overheard the LT and the sarge talking about you. They're finna get you out of here today. Do you need me to do anything for you before you leave?"

"Nah, bro, but thank you so much for everything, Myles. Especially the coffee. I know you're not supposed to bring any shit in here for us anyway." Freddy paused. "And it looks like I skeeted that investigation!"

Myles laughed and replied, "Anytime, my dude. I got my picks and chooses who I look out for. A chunk of these guys are in protective custody or snitching on somebody anyway. But yo, since the investigation's over, what the fuck happened to you?"

Freddy thought about it. He knows the consequences of letting a lame know too much.

"You know I fuck with you, so I'll give you a little rundown of what happened," said Freddy.

*****

Lyon Lake: Dorm 3, June 30

About two and a half months ago, Freddy sat alone in his two-man cell, minding his own business, listening to the radio while the other inmates were out on recreation moving freely around the unit. Freddy's door had been left cracked because he has been in and out of the cell a few times already. Big mistake.

Freddy was almost in a meditative state when three inmates barged through his door, all of them holding a weapon of some sort.

"You know what time it is. Tell us where the dope's at," one of the goons said.

The first thing Freddy noticed about the goons was that they all had five-point stars tattooed on their arms. He also saw tattoos of a handprint and the word "Mob" in big bold letters.

Bloods.

Very slowly, Freddy got off the bed and put his back to the wall.

The leader of the group held out a long knife made out of scrap metal and cornered Freddy while the other two snooped around the cell. Freddy knew better than to do anything stupid, so he observed their faces very carefully. Freddy recognized one of the snoops. He was the one that Freddy caught fucking a punk in the shower a few days ago. This all makes sense now.

Freddy stared the knife man down hard. Freddy could tell by looking at the man that he was a bit frightened and didn't want to do this job.

"This dude doesn't have shit! I can't believe you talked us into this shit," the first snoop said and gave a little shove to the under-cover gay boy.

The first snoop stomped his way out of the cell angry then followed the gay boy, leaving the knife man alone with Freddy.

Some brothers, Freddy thought to himself.

The knife man backed up slowly toward the door, but very quickly, Freddy shoved him toward the other wall and ran and shut the door. The doors lock from the outside so nobody could help the knife man. Before the knife man had time to react, Freddy jumped at him like a flying wombat, automatically pinning him to the ground. Freddy hit him numerous times with his palms like a karate kid to avoid getting any type of damage to his knuckles.

He was out cold. Unconscious as fuck.

Then Freddy started stripping knife man's clothes down to his boxers. Freddy took his state shirt, pants, and his white undershirt and pressed them up to his poor, defenseless upper half of his body. Freddy got on the knife man's shoulders and got extremely close to his face. Close enough to kiss him. He tilted the poor man's head to the side and began taking a bite of his ear. Freddy really had to chomp hard and gnawed his ear off. Freddy then chewed it up and swallowed it.

"I'm going to shit you out, biatch!" Freddy said out loud.

All of the blood that was gushing out of his ear was now leaking all over his clothes that Freddy pushed up against him. Then Freddy took the knife off the floor and stabbed the man one good time in the heart, putting the delicate man out of his misery. Freddy looked out the window of his cell. Most of the inmate movement in the unit depleted. Freddy was patient.

Once chow was called for the dorm, Freddy waited for each inmate to leave the building. If Freddy wants to pull this homicide off, he would have to miss this chow call. To hell with it! He already ate his dinner. Once the coast was clear, he put surgical gloves on and began dragging the body out of his cell. Toward the shower they go.

Once Freddy got the body in the shower, he cut the water on and threw his bloody clothes over the railing to make it look like someone was showering. Freddy then wiped off his fingerprints that were on the knife while it was still lodged in the body's chest. The body will not be found until later that night. So in the meantime, Freddy took a brand-new mop and raw bleach and began thoroughly cleaning his room. There wasn't any blood on the floor anyway, but Freddy wasn't taking any chances. Freddy then disposed of the gloves and all of the cleaning materials.

*****

"And that's a rundown of what happened, Myles," Freddy said.

"Holy shit, dude, that was smack nasty! But wait, what did you do when you caught that dude in the shower fucking that punk?" Myles asked.

"Oh, I forgot to mention that part. I filled up a small bag of ice and dumped it into my bucket. Then I took three bags of milk that I have been saving for a couple months and poured it into the bucket. Yes, the milk was very chunky and spoiled." Freddy smiled. "Then I put some state juice in it. Then I pissed in it. By then the bucket was only halfway full, so I just topped the rest of it off with water…and I dumped it on them. Once I did that, I ran inside the punk's room and stole all of his homemade li'l bitch clothes. Shirts and stockings and shit."

"What the fuck do you plan on doing with those?" Myles asked.

"Things," Freddy said. "And I believe that's why those boys tried to get me. The undercover gay boy felt some type of way that I caught him violating, so he told his brothers I was the dope man. He probably threw other dirt on my name too. I really don't have anything against the gang members either. It's wrong to judge a whole group by the acts of a couple people, but I still had to handle business. I should have fucked him."

"I think I've heard enough. We get it. You are *smack nasty!*" Myles said.

Freddy likes that expression a lot.

"Mr. Dawson, pack up. You're going back to the yard!" an officer yelled down the corridor.

CHAPTER 2

Freddy began gathering up all of his things. Not that there was much anyway. In lockup, you are completely stripped down to the bare necessities with no canteen. After he packed up, he picked up all of his trash that was left in his cell to save Myles from having to do it. Freddy headed down the corridor with his small net bag of clothes that the officers let him have. He approached the control room where LT Hickenbottom was waiting. Myles was in the presence as well.

"Dawson, all of your personal property is in this green duffel bag. I need you to take it all out the bag and load up all your stuff in the buggie over there." And pointed at it.

"I don't need that buggie. Watch what I do," Freddy replied.

Freddy went in his net bag and dug out a bedsheet and spread it out on the floor. He then took the green duffel bag, opened it, and dumped all of his property on the sheet. He then tied up all of the corners of the sheet making one large bag.

"All right, Dawson, before you leave, I need you to sign a couple papers. The first one states that you do not need any protective custody and can be mixed in with the general population, and the other paper states that you received all of your property."

Freddy grabbed the pen off the table and signed the papers without question. "What dorm do I go to, LT?" Freddy asked.

"You are going to unit six. It's the only place with an open bed right now," Hickenbottom replied.

Freddy knew that was bullshit but whatever.

"Officer Clardy is waiting outside the building, Dawson. She's going to take you to six. Now get out."

Freddy looked him in the eye and slowly walked to the glass door where he saw the socially awkward-looking chick waiting on him.

Myles jumped in the way. "Yo, yo! Be safe, my dude. If you need me for anything, you know where I'm at. Also, when you get to six, holla at my boy, Tweak. He's a fucking beast with that tat gun. Let him know I sent you." Myles then got out of Freddy's way and smiled.

"Will do, bruh. See you later. Catch me on the yard."

Freddy exited the building with his bag and began walking with Clardy, neither of them speaking a word. This is indeed about to be an awkward long walk. They walked through operations then on a long sidewalk leading up to a massive staircase followed by a rocky dirt road, where the big trucks drive on to deliver wood to a plant within the prison.

Freddy couldn't take it anymore. He finally broke the ice. "Are we anywhere close yet? How much farth—"

Clardy cut him short. "Oh, we are getting close. We have to walk around this other lockup building, past the bus stop, then walk through the sally port and the gates, and then we will be there. Ugh, I didn't do my hair right this morning. I look like a wreck. This fucking job treats me like shit. Oh my god, my mom is going to kill me. I forgot to mail out that card for her this morning. My shoes are so uncomfortable. We need to sit down at the bus stop for a minute when we get there. I need a rest," Clardy expressed a mile a minute.

Oh my fucking god, what is wrong with this bitch? Freddy thought to himself. *I shoulda kept my ass quiet.*

The whole walk to the bus stop Clardy just kept yappin' and yappin' with no breaks…or brakes.

"I need some drugs," Freddy said out loud. Joking but almost serious.

Clardy jumped back, "Why didn't you just say so? I already know all about you, Dawson. I'll see what I can do for you. I am a routine officer in six. But god, I hate it so much. None of the other officers will work up there so administration makes me run it. This is by far the worst dorm."

Freddy was so shocked; he had no idea what to say, but he was relieved to finally make it to the bus stop where he can set down his property and rest with the crazy lady for a minute.

They both got really quiet again.

Freddy was thinking to himself, *What the fuck is going on?*

After a fast couple of minutes, Clardy got up and said, "Okay, I'm ready."

The duo approached the first gate that had to be unlocked with a key. It took Clady a minute to find the right one.

"Aha!" she said aloud. "Forward we go."

Freddy groaned.

They proceeded up a slight hill where there stood another gate. Beyond this gate was a sally port with a gatehouse leading toward the parking lot of the entire prison compound over toward the left, but straight ahead, there were two more gates leading to Freddy's new dorm.

Holy shit! There's no way these people are moving me to a place that is so close to the streets. I can dip outta this bitch! Idiots, I swear! Freddy was thinking to himself.

"I don't have a key for these gates. I have to call the gatehouse on my radio, and the new girl will pop them open with the push of a button," Clardy said with a smile. She hit her radio, "Ninety-three, thirty-six. Pop gates three, two, and one."

Freddy paid attention to these numbers.

The first gate popped, and they walked across the sally port just to find that the other two gates were still locked.

"Ugh! Freakin' trainee!" Clardy said.

"Ninety-three, thirty-six. Gates two and one please."

After an awkward pause, both gates finally popped, and Freddy advanced forward to his new temporary home.

"You will be going to room thirteen, Dawson. Good luck and I will see you soon." Clardy shut the gate behind Freddy while she went into the gatehouse, leaving Freddy to join the mix.

CHAPTER 3

10:25 a.m.

As soon as Freddy walked in the building, he noticed his sur-roundings. There were no doors to the cells. It was all open with each cell having a six-foot privacy wall going around the cells, so you can at least have *some* privacy. The dorm had a high resemblance to a large office with cubicles for their employees.

Freddy stopped an inmate that had just left his cube and was now walking his way. This man looked like a heavy mental health patient.

"Yo dude, what the hell is this place?" Freddy asked.

"Out of eleven dorms, two lockups, and a step-down program on this yard, this is the only motherfucking open dorm. It took me a while to get used to it. I call this place the pleasure palace. Don't get caught up smoking that K2!" the man said.

Freddy already knew what time it was considering how long he has been doing time.

Freddy had to ask, "Are you mental health?"

"Yes. Most of us are. Prozac, Zoloft, Thorazine, Seroquel, Trazadone…you name it, we got it!"

"I think I got the message," Freddy replied.

With his property, Freddy took a glance down the first hallway looking for his new room, lucky thirteen.

Nope. He walked to the next hallway.

Still nope. He backtracked and found the door leading to the other side of the dorm. On the door, it said, "South side," so he must be on the north side.

He opened the door going to the south side and walked into the main area. It was a mirror reflection of the side he was just on. He looked down the first hall. There it was.

The first fucking room.

Fucking Christ, Freddy thought and stepped in the room.

The first thing Freddy saw was the little Korean boy he had as a roommate. Eighteen, maybe nineteen. He was asleep. As Freddy set his belongings down, it woke up the Korean boy.

Freddy walked up to him and whispered in his ear, "Shh, go back to sleep. This will be over before you know it."

The boy was so frightened, he rolled over and pulled the blanket over his head.

Freddy found the boy's prison ID hanging on his locker. He then used his photographic memory to remember his legal name and inmate number, so he can be checked out. Ho Chen Xu. Easy to remember.

Freddy opened up his sack of property and looked for his roll of industrial tape. Once he found it, he set it on his new bunk. He then found his very thick manilla envelope in the trenches of his property. He opened up the envelope and took out a very large poster of Pat Sajak that was nearly the same size as his privacy wall. Very carefully, Freddy taped his poster of the *Wheel of Fortune* alum to the wall so neatly and perfectly that there were no wrinkles or crevices in the picture at all. For the rest of Ho Chen Xu's bid, he would be stared at by Pat Sajak. Freddy took a step back and admired the poster.

"Mmmm," he mumbled out. "I'll unpack the rest of this shit later, I got things to do," Freddy whispered to himself.

Freddy left the room and stepped into the main area once again, where he found the prison wall phones so that he can call the only person out there in the world that he can trust, his twin sister, Starlene.

Freddy picked up the phone.

"Press one for a debit call. Press zero for a collect or prepaid call," a female robot said.

Freddy pressed zero.

Star was always good about keeping money on the phone.

Then Freddy dialed her phone number.

"Please enter your inmate number and four-digit pin," the robot said.

Freddy did so.

"Please say your first and last name after the beep."

"Freddy Dawson," Freddy said in a monotone manner.

"Please confirm your first and last name after the beep."

"Freddy Dawson," he said once again.

"Your name does not match. Please try again. Please say your first and last name after the beep."

Freddy cleared his throat and spoke a little louder, "Freddy Dawson."

And again at the beep.

"Freddy Dawson."

"You name does not match. Please try your call again later." And the robot hung up.

"Fuck!" Freddy yelled out, and the whole dorm went quiet.

Freddy picked up the phone again and repeated the same process, except this time, he screamed his name into the phone.

"Freddy Dawson!" he yelled after the beep.

All of the inmates at this time were sticking their heads out of their cubicle, wondering what all the commotion was about. At least they all know Freddy's name now.

"Freddy Dawson!" he screamed for the confirmation.

There was a long pause. Freddy looked down his hallway and saw all of the inmates staring at him in confusion.

Freddy raised his hand and shoulder in an annoyed manner and yelled out, "What's the problem!"

And all of the inmates carried on with their business.

The robot finally replied, "Thank you for using Inmate Telephone Services. Your call will be connected."

Freddy mumbled to himself, "People wonder why I'm a serial killer."

Starlene picked up on the first ring, which she usually does. And instead of listening to the robot give her all of the bullshit options, she went ahead and pressed one to accept the call.

"Thank you for using our services. Your conversation may begin now," the robot said.

Starlene was the first to speak, "Hey, twin! Where have you been? You usually don't wait this long to call."

"I can't even begin to tell you. It was hell. But I need you to do something for me if you can. I need you to look up my new room-mate on the state's website and tell me his charges." Freddy gave Star Xu's information.

"Okay," she replied, and there was a pause.

"It appears that his charges are fraud and money laundering. Both are second offences. His max-out date is in about six months," Star said.

"Those sound like federal charges. I wonder what he's doing in the state prison and not the federal prison system. Can you google his name and see if anything comes up?" Freddy asked.

"Sure."

And another pause.

"Okay. This is what I found. It says Columbia, South Carolina, man accused of fraud for the distribution and product of illicit and illegal coupons. The police confiscated a Mercedes-Benz and a yacht that Xu had owned and stashed in a large storage garage about fifteen miles from his residence," Star said and giggled.

"That's all I needed to know, sis," Freddy said.

"So what are you going to do now, Freddy?"

"I'm going to get my man. But first I'm going to teach him a few life lessons," Freddy said and hung up.

CHAPTER 4

Once Freddy hung up the phone, he walked over to the water fountain, which was just a few feet away, and got himself a little sip of water when the overhead intercom went off.

"Attention in the area. Mr. Johnson's GED class for today is cancelled. Also, Mr. Peter and Mr. Floyd's classes are cancelled as well," a man's voice said.

Freddy got the attention of a bystander. "Who are those people?" Freddy asked.

"They are over education. The last two you heard teach auto mechanics and brick masonry, but they won't do you any good whatsoever. The classes get cancelled damn near every day. You'll see, pilgrim." And the man pointed his finger at Freddy's face.

Freddy just slowly backed up, turned around, and walked back to his room where Xu was awake and rummaging through his locker.

Freddy broke the ice, "What's up, little dude?"

"Nothing much. Did you just come from another dorm?"

Freddy did not want Xu to know he just got out of lockup, so Freddy did not lie to him but didn't tell the full truth either.

"I just came from the lower yard. My name's Freddy."

"Everyone at home calls me Kim. It is a traditional name in my ancestry and culture. I am new to the yard and, well, prison in general. I have six months left."

"That's cool. I don't have that much time left either," Freddy lied.

Freddy began unpacking his property and started setting up his locker while carrying on the conversation.

"When do we go eat for lunch?" Freddy asked.

"About two hours, I think. You have time to finish what you're doing."

"Has anybody been giving you any problems, Kim?"

"Yes and no. I really try to stay to myself, except there have been a few guys approach me in a very friendly and uncomfortable manner talking about, 'Oh, anywhere you go in this life, you need to be yourself, and oh, I am such a savage.' Things like that. I think they want to know if I'm gay or not. And they keep asking me to smoke that K2 stuff!"

Freddy thought of an idea. "This is what I'm going to do for you, Kim. After they call for chow, I'm going to show you who else is gay. Most of them are undercover and like to pry on younger dudes like yourself because they believe you won't stand up for yourself." Freddy was hiding his true intentions toward Kim.

Kim was being buttered up and doesn't even know it.

"Thanks, man, just let me know when you're ready," Kim said.

After Freddy finished unpacking and got his living area straightened up, he relaxed and took a little cat nap. He was shortly awakened by the call for chow.

Freddy quickly got out of bed and threw on his state inmate shirt and pants and slipped on his shoes. Time to network a little bit. He went outside and stood with the group of inmates leaving out with him at the first gate.

Clardy came out of the gatehouse as gates one and two popped open. The inmates stampeded but got stuck at the third gate. They were just like a herd of cattle.

"Ugh!" Clardy moaned out. "Ninety-three, thirty-six. Gate three." You could tell Clardy was a little overwhelmed because she forgot to hit the button on her radio.

An inmate had to tell her what she had done. She got frustrated and pushed the button. But before she got to say anything, the gate popped.

"This is unbelievable," Clardy cried out.

As the inmates plowed through gate three, Clardy got the attention of Freddy in a low-key manner so that the other inmates would not suspect anything. Freddy slowed down his pace as he was about to walk by her.

"I need to talk to you later, Dawson," Clardy whispered in Freddy's ear as he walked by.

He nodded and continued on.

Clardy walked down the steep hill to manually unlock the final gate. Once she did, the inmates got louder and advanced through the gate and onward to the yard.

After walking by countless institutional buildings, a couple industrial plants, and a maintenance shop, Freddy noticed a junkyard off the side of the walking path to the kitchen. There was nothing but a bunch of useless scrap metal, trash, old light bulbs, and bullshit that just got thrown away. Freddy slipped away, unnoticed from the crowd, and went around the fence and into the head of the junkyard. Without wanting to get caught, he quickly grabbed the easiest and most accessible piece of metal he could find. It was almost perfect. It was long, but not too long, and somewhat sharp. Freddy would have to do some work to it, but it'll do for now. He lodged his new weapon in his pants around the waistband, so it wouldn't fall out while he was walking and jumped in the back of the line without being detected.

Smooth.

Inside the kitchen, someone in the line spoke out loud, "What's on the trays?"

"It's a moon rock again!" a kitchen worker yelled back.

A moon rock is an uncooked blob of meat with onions inside it. It is usually served with watered-down mashed potatoes and a piece of corn bread that nobody ever eats. If you are that corn bread, something was truly wrong with you.

Once Freddy got his tray, he looked for a table to sit at, so he could enjoy his corn bread. There were only two available tables for him to choose from. The first table sat an old-school Black gentleman, and the other table did not have anybody sitting at it at all. Given Freddy was somewhat of an antisocial person, he chose the empty table. He did not have anything negative against the old man; he just wanted to be alone.

Huge mistake.

As soon as Freddy took a seat, three crazy-looking White guys with Hitler Nazi symbol tattoos on them swarmed the table with condiments in their hands, making Freddy extremely uncomfortable.

"Hey, brother, you need some salt?"

"How about hot sauce?"

"Ketchup?" all three of them said in almost unison with big smiles on their faces.

The disturbance they were causing made a lot of the inmates around them looking and being nosy. Being nosy is what the typical inmate does best. Freddy had to make a fast decision.

He got up and looked at the man holding the ketchup and said, "No, thank you. Would you like some lip gloss and mascara? You would look good with it." Freddy shoved the corn bread in his mouth and started heading toward the exit, leaving his tray at the table.

The Nazis will never talk to Freddy again.

From now on, Freddy will make better decisions where he sits.

Once Freddy got outside, he turned the corner and waited for the ketchup man to come out. It did not take long, and he came out by himself for some reason. Freddy had to make his move before the other two come out. As the ketchup man started walking, Freddy appeared from around the corner and tapped his shoulder.

"Hey, man, I just wanted to apologize for the things I said to you in there and walking out. That was very rude of me," Freddy said.

Startled from the awkward approach, the ketchup man replied, "Yeah, you had me tripping. Hell, I've already been up for eight days straight, and I thought I was hearing shit. Even my brothers are too scared to come out right now. They said they can't trust it right now."

Freddy looked at him in wonder and then said, "Everything's cool but I need to tell you something. I'm a leader and not a follower, but if you would like to follow me to the blind spot over by the maintenance shop, I have something for you." Freddy felt the man was paranoid.

"I'm not a motherfucking snitch if that's what you're trying to say," the ketchup man finally blurted out.

"I never said you were. I do ice. Do you?" Freddy lied.

The man's eyes grew wide, and he nodded his head fast.

"Come on then, let's go do us a line," Freddy said and led him off the yard and to the blind spot where nobody could see them.

On arrival, Freddy pulled out his metal weapon from his waistband, but the ketchup man did not see it because he was behind Freddy. The weapon was not exactly sharp enough to piece the skin, but he could still do some damage. Freddy turned around, revealing his weapon.

The man looked at it and yelled, "Hey, I told you I wasn't a fucking snit—"

The man's rebuttal was cut short due to a blow to the head with the weapon. It wasn't hard enough to put him to sleep, but it was enough to make the man give in to Freddy's needs.

"Why did you do that?" the man asked, hurt and on the ground.

"Shut up and turn around. And take off your fucking clothes, bitch," Freddy said angrily.

Freddy proceeded to fuck him, dry.

While thrusting, Freddy said, "This'll make you stay up eight more days!"

When finished, the smug Freddy headed back to his dorm to accommodate Kim, leaving the ketchup man on the ground scarred for life as he was mumbling unintelligent things.

CHAPTER 5

Once Freddy got inside the dorm, he put the things he brought to the kitchen with him to his room, got his soap and other shower material, and took a hot shower.

When it was count time, Freddy was already in his room, drying his feet off and applying hygiene. He took a second to speak to Kim.

"Kim, when the count clears, I'm going to have you go sit in the dayroom. I'll be a few minutes, but I'll be coming right behind you. Remember what we talked about earlier? I'm going to show you some punks," Freddy said. "They are having a big poker game."

"All right, I am ready," Kim replied.

After about forty-five minutes later, the count cleared, and Kim proceeded to the dayroom.

"I'll be as fast as I can," Freddy said to himself.

He revealed a net bag full of clothes and miscellaneous items from under his locker and dumped everything onto the floor. Freddy usually kept his things organized but did not have time to whenever he was leaving lockup. He rummaged through everything and threw aside all of the girly clothes and makeup he stole from the he-she in dorm three and threw everything else back into the net bag.

Then he began to put on some of the makeup. Heavy on the mascara, light on lip gloss. Then he applied some kind of oil to his face to make it shiny. Then he picked up what appears to be a mini-skirt and a crop top.

"This will have to do."

He changed out of his state clothes and into his bitch clothes. It was a very tight fit.

Freddy thought about shaving his legs and said, "Nah, these motherfuckers are straight savages. No need." Almost satisfied with the brief transformation, he put a beanie over his head to cover up his hair.

Time for action.

After a short walk, Freddy posted up in the doorway of the dayroom, strongly resembling a slutty whore to the best of his ability, and listened to a conversation they were having at the poker table.

"Hell naw, fuck the police! I'll never go on PC. I'm only down twenty dollars. Matter fact, house man, give me ten more dollars!" a man named Foot yelled while the others were laughing.

Kim looked up and saw what Freddy had done to himself and tried not to laugh.

Freddy cleared his throat. "Ahem, hey boys. I'm on the lookout for somebody. I'm fresh out of lockup!"

Freddy began waving his hand over his face as if he was hot and rolled his eyes over to the poker table.

"What the fuck?" Foot screamed out as he looked back, losing the hand he was just dealt.

"Get the fuck outta here, you AIDS-infested faggot! Nobody in here wants to hear that shit! You can go somewhere else with that shit!" Foot said out loud.

"I'll see you soon, big boy," Freddy replied in a seductive manner and went back to his room to change back into his normal clothes.

Kim came back shortly after that.

"Holy shit, Freddy, you're crazy!" Kim said.

"But I'm not. Let's drink a cup of coffee tonight and stay up a little late. Let's see if I reeled a fish."

*****

Later that night and after some strong cups of coffee, Freddy and Kim stayed up and bonded a little bit.

"See, it's the same motherfuckers who claim they have wife and kids at home, a hot girlfriend that live a bachelor-style life out there in the world that are low-key punks. They catch a little five- or six-year bid and then have to explain to their families how they caught AIDS in prison. Some people probably wouldn't tell them at all and just go around spreading the shit," Freddy ranted.

Kim sat back and listened to his mentor.

"This is what I want you to do, Kim. Here in a couple minutes, I want you to get in the bed and act like you're asleep. Stay on point though because I have a feeling we will have a visitor tonight," Freddy instructed.

Kim nodded and did what he was told.

At this point, Freddy believed that if he told Kim to jump off a building headfirst that he would do it.

Once Kim got in his bed, Freddy followed suit. And there they laid quietly and in the dark.

A little bit past midnight, a head poked in the room from behind the wall. Freddy looked up at him. And there and behold, Foot appeared in the doorway and gave Freddy a let's-go motion and pointed the other direction.

Freddy got up out of bed and began to follow Foot. Freddy quickly glanced back at Kim to make sure he just witnessed all this, which he did.

Freddy then followed Foot into the bathroom then into the shower area. Foot hung up his shower material on the curtain's rail to try to fool anybody who may walk into the bathroom this late at night so that they would think he was showering. He must have done this before.

With both of them entering the same shower, Freddy got in front of Foot and acted like he was bending over for him. As soon as Foot got close, Freddy quickly stood, busting Foot in between the eyes followed by a couple punches and a kick in the testicles. Foot was rolling and squirming on the pissy shower floor in incredible pain.

Freddy got out of the shower and ran to the head of the bathroom and got the broom. He went back to Foot, who was trying to get himself back up again. Freddy stopped him by hitting him in the head with the broomstick, knocking him out for a short period. Freddy then rolled Foot onto his back and stuck the broomstick barely in his mouth, so it looked like he was sucking on it. Freddy then took Foot's arms and wrapped them around the entire broom, so it looked like he was making sweet love to the broom on the shower floor.

Freddy stormed out of the bedroom and told Kim, who still was waiting in the bed, to go look at Foot. Kim sprang up.

"Wait!" Freddy whispered loudly. "Once you take a good look at him, go up to the officer station and tell the police that there's a shot-out motherfucker on the shower floor that needs assistance."

Kim nodded and proceeded to the bathroom.

As he entered, Freddy stood in the main common area to watch the ceremony that was about to unfold. Kim came out of the bathroom smiling and gave Freddy a thumbs-up as he walked over to the officer station.

Moments later, the officer appeared and went into the bathroom.

"Oh my god," Freddy heard from far away.

Freddy poked his head in the bathroom first and saw the officer abetting Foot. So Freddy entered the bathroom to pretend that he was washing his hands. The officer must have woken Foot up because Freddy heard him mumbling.

"Foot, you know I have to write you up and log this in an incident report this time. I'm tired of giving you chances," the police said.

It's bad when the police know your nickname.

"I need protective custody. I can't be in here anymore," Foot said, sitting upright on the shower floor now.

The police laughed and got on his radio. "Operations thirty-six. I got one that needs PC. I'm sending him to the holding cell." The officer got off the radio and just looked at Foot, who looked very embarrassed. "You must have ran up a nice little bill this time. I know you, Foot, you staged this entire scene just so you could make a slick getaway. But what do I know? All I do is serve and protect. And I'm still writing this up and charging you."

"I need a mental evaluation," Foot mumbled.

Freddy scurried out of the bathroom and went back to the room.

Freddy and Kim sat quietly until they heard the front door open and close.

"They must be gone now. Did you enjoy the show, Kim?"

"I have never seen anything like it."

"You haven't seen anything."

CHAPTER 6

Freddy and Kim slept in for a good portion of the morning considering how late they stayed up.

The overhead intercom woke them both up. "May I have your attention! All education is closed," the lady in the intercom announced.

"Again?" Freddy mumbled as he was rolling out of bed.

Freddy will now begin his eventful day.

As he started doing his little morning routines, the intercom went off again.

"EDUCATION IS CLOSED! DO NOT REPORT OR YOU WILL BE CHARGED WITH OUT OF PLACE!" the lady screamed.

"Are you serious? What type of shit are these people on? Whatever it is, it has to end with a -ine. Any meds with a -ine can't be good for you. How do you get written up for wanting to get an education?" Freddy ranted to Kim.

"Did you use to be on meds, Freddy?" Kim asked.

"No. I mean, maybe. I really don't know. My brain is jelly now."

As Freddy stepped out of his room, he heard a buggie being pushed through the front door. Someone was moving in. As Freddy proceeded toward the buggie, Myles appeared in the doorway and was greeted.

"Holy shit, Myles! You're moving in?" Freddy asked, a big smile on his face.

"Yes, sir. They asked me if I wanted to come up here, and I said fuck it. I was getting burnt out in that other dorm and needed a change of scenery. Plus, I'm going to pull up on Tweak and get tatted.

I will put you in the car too, Freddy. So be thinking about what you want done."

Freddy already knows. He grew excited. "Pull up on me first quarter then, Myles. I'll be waiting."

"Damn, let me unpack first," Myles rebutted.

Freddy was ecstatic. Ever since he had been doing time, he has never really had a friend. Myles was the only person he could vibe with and did not have to worry about bullshit hitting the fan.

While waiting for Myles, Freddy figured that he would get a head start by making the tattoo ink. He walked into a child molester's room and took a soda from under his bed while he was watching TV. As Freddy left the room, the man just looked at him without saying a word. Freddy popped the soda and turned around back toward the child molester.

"Next time you should just kill the kid. You would have earned more respect with a murder charge as opposed to fondling their no-no spots. Isn't life weird?" Freddy cocked his head and smiled and chugged the entire soda in front of the man.

He still did not get a response. Freddy has a very sick mind, but there was still some truth to what he said at times.

Freddy took the empty can to his room. He turned the can upside down on the floor so that the bottom of the can faced upward. He then took a big scoop of petroleum jelly with his fingers and filled up the bottom of the soda can with the jelly.

"Fucking Christ!" Freddy wailed out as he got petroleum jelly all over his hands. "I can't fucking stand this shit! It gets all over the fucking place, and it's too hard to clean up!" Freddy yelled as he threw the whole tub of petroleum jelly at the wall, exploding on impact. "Clean this shit up, Kim. But not now. Wait until I leave before this stupid jelly gives me a heart attack."

Kim had no idea how to respond to this, so he just remained silent.

Freddy then took some tissue, folded it up and twisted it until it looked like a nub, and jammed it in the center of the jelly that was on the soda can. He then built a cone out of paper using toothpaste to hold the cone together and set the can inside the cone. Time to make fire. Freddy broke a razor and disassembled the razor blade. He found a broken pencil in his locker and began trying to lodge the razor blade into the bottom of the broken pencil so that the blade was touching the pencil's graphite. Once accomplished, he stuck the razor with the pencil stuck to it into the left side of an electrical socket. He then asked Kim if he had a wire.

"Will a bread tie work? That's the only kind of wire I have," Kim said.

"Perfect."

Freddy twisted up another piece of tissue. He will be using this one as a wick. He then took the bread tie, stuck one end of it in the right side of the socket, held his tissue up by the pencil, and carefully touched the graphite with the other end of the bread tie, which produced a spark, setting the piece of tissue on fire. He took his flame over to the can, picked up the cone, and lit the piece of tissue that was shoved in the petroleum jelly and carefully placed the cone back over it, holding it steady so it does not fall over. Once balanced, Freddy found a piece of cardboard paper and placed it on top of the cone so that the burning smoke sut would stick to the construction paper. It would take about thirty minutes for it to stop smoking, so in the meantime, Freddy will be sharpening his knife. Once the smoke stopped, he picked up the construction paper and used a playing card to scrape all the black sut the petroleum jelly has made into a small, clear container.

All done.

The timing was perfect because Freddy saw Myles pacing the floors.

"Oh, Freddy, there you are. I didn't know what room you stayed in. You ready?"

"Yeah. And I made the ink for both of us too."

"Hell yeah. That saves us a lot of time, plus it's a good shift. There's a decent officer working. Come on, Tweak already made the gun, and he is twacked out on ice right now. He's ready to go," Myles said.

They proceeded to Tweak's room, Myles leading the way since Freddy did not know who he was or where he lived.

Upon arrival, the first thing Freddy noticed about Tweak was his teardrop tattoo underneath his nose. Before introducing himself, Freddy asked him what that tattoo meant.

"Every time that I cry, I let the teardrops fall all the way down my face before I wipe them. I don't have to reach as far," Tweak said with a very serious facial expression.

"Well, okay then," Freddy said while looking at Myles.

"Nice to meet you, Freddy. I'm putting you in the chair first because Myles is getting a big piece. What do you want?"

"I want 'SMACK NASTY' underneath my belly button. This is my first tattoo," Freddy admitted.

"Woah. Are you sure you want to start there, dude? That's a pretty painful spot to get tatted, let alone your first."

"I'll be all right. Just tell me what I owe you."

"I'll tell you what, shoot by the chapel tomorrow morning during service and look for somebody named Eggshell. He has a package for me. Go get it and bring it to me. He'll break you off too," Tweak ordered.

"What does he look like?"

"Just ask around. He works there. Come on, lay down and take your shirt off. I'm ready to go." Tweak took the ink sut out of Freddy's hand and dumped a little bit of it in a toothpaste cap.

He then took a chunk of non-powder deodorant with his fingers and wrapped it in a silky cloth he made out of a white T-shirt. He squeezed on the deodorant until the alcohol dripped into the toothpaste cap with the sut. After about five drops, the sut turned into the perfect substitute of real tattoo ink.

"I am free handing this and it is going to hurt."

Freddy silently just laid there, not even ready for the pain he is about to endure. Tweak cranked up the gun and as soon as the needle touched Freddy's skin, he yelled out and grabbed Tweak's wrist.

"Aah, you son of a bitch!" Freddy cried out.

Myles jumped in. "Freddy, chill out and take a breather. It's too late to turn back, so you might as well thug it out."

"My bad. Okay, for real this time."

Tweak got back to work with Freddy cooperating this time.

*****

Once finished, Freddy was in excruciating pain, but it was well paid off. The smack nasty tattoo was flawless.

"All right, Freddy. Get yourself cleaned up and don't forget to do that in the morning!" Tweak said, smiling.

Freddy did so, knowing tomorrow was going to be a busy day.

When nighttime, came it was time for the officer's shift change.

*****

Freddy was hanging around in the main common area, conversating with a couple inmates. Officer Clardy came into the dorm with her backpack, prepared to work the night shift. Clardy looked at Freddy, flashing him a seductive gaze before she went to the office.

CHAPTER 7

It had been a long day. All the inmates were tired from working hard at various yard jobs. It was pretty much free labor, except if you had an industry job where you could make a chump-change hourly wage. But then you would have to deal with the hazardous environment like getting your fingers sawed off or breathing in wood dust and other chemicals to damage your lungs. Then there would be deductions in your paycheck such as victim's awareness, child support, room and board, and things like that, even if you don't have a victim in the crime you are convicted. But it was still money. Money that could be legally earned as an inmate, and therefore a lot of inmates have this job. They put in very long hours of shifts too. Sometimes twelve to fourteen hours. So long story short, the inmates are tired.

But not Freddy.

Clardy was conducting the nine-o'clock roll call count. Once she was finished, most inmates were getting some shut-eye. Once Clardy was finished, she went back to the office and turned the lights off so nobody could pry on her because for a socially awkward female in a men's prison, she could be a target. And for some reason, she looked pretty damn good tonight.

Freddy remembered that she needed to talk to him. She had mentioned that to him on his way to the kitchen yesterday. So once Freddy believed the inmates were asleep, he crept up to the office door and knocked on it.

Clardy reached across the desk and turned the knob for Freddy to enter. The first thing Freddy noticed was that Clardy was not wearing her stab-proof vest, revealing some of her cleavage, with her buttoned-up shirt with the top two buttons unbuttoned. She even applied more makeup, more than which she came in with, and lastly instead of having her hair tied up, she let it hang loosely. She looked excited to see Freddy.

"Hey, Dawson! Shut that door behind you, I don't want anybody being nosy."

Freddy did so.

Without any small talk, Clardy walked around the desk and embraced Freddy. She put her hand on his chest. "I want you, Dawson. I've missed you," she said in a soft, seductive tone.

"Yeah? What was that you wanted to tell me yes—"

"Fuck me," she cut him short.

She took Freddy's arm and pulled him into the officer bathroom in the middle of the office and shut the door behind them.

Freddy did not know how to act. He was not used to any females in general seducing him. He had grown up in prison, and for some reason, the prison system did not want you near any females. It was probably the diabolical works of some faggot politicians. Freddy had always wondered how real pussy was, but he was caught out of his comfort zone, so he needed to say something and fast.

"I'll tell you what, Clardy. Take your makeup off and make yourself look like a dude, and I will fuck your brains out," Freddy said.

She looked at him mysteriously but then began to comply. "Kinky, huh? I think I like that. Step outside for a minute, and I'll dude myself up for you," she said.

Freddy stepped out for a couple minutes and reentered and saw that she really tried to look like a man but didn't do that great of a job.

"What do you think?" Clardy asked, looking down at herself.

"It'll have to do. And one more thing. Shut your fucking mouth and let me do all of the work!"

They began to undress. Upon instinct, Freddy bent her over and went straight for her butthole.

"Ahh! What are you doing!" she cried.

Freddy stopped himself once he realized what he had just done.

"My bad, bro, turn around then and let me see that pussy!" He flipped her around and began penetrating her pussy.

"Woah," Freddy said while thrusting. "I didn't know which hole I like more."

After a few minutes of hot sex, Freddy finished and came all inside of her.

"Mmm, you can fuck my ass now if you would like," Clardy suggested.

"It's over with now, bitch. You should have said something. Now put your clothes back on."

They got dressed and came out of the bathroom. Freddy began to leave the office but got stopped.

"Oh, Dawson! Wait up!" She reached behind the desk. "Look, I wasn't able to get any drugs, but I was able to get this."

Clardy presented a touch screen cell phone and charger to Freddy.

"Take it, Dawson, I already put the first month's plan on it for you. Hee hee," she giggled.

The first and the last plan, Freddy thought. "Well, thank you, Clardy. This is awfully kind of you. If you need me again, you know where I'm at. I'm going to use the phone really fast and call it a night. I have a busy day tomorrow."

"Be safe, Freddy. Whoops, I mean Dawson. Have a good night and I'll see you again soon."

Freddy left the office with the phone.

*****

Freddy stopped by his room and hid the charger underneath the pillow. He then turned the phone on, set his own password to unlock it, and turned the volume down on it. Freddy could get in big trouble if he was caught with a cell phone. He had to be precautious and not let anybody see it.

Freddy left his room and proceeded to the bathroom with his new toy. Once he went inside, he went into the little cutoff at the end of the bathroom and sat on the bench. Nobody would be able to see him there. He unlocked his phone and dialed his sister's phone number.

She answered after the first ring. "Hello?" a tired Starlene said.

"Twin, it's me. I need to tell you something."

"Wait," she responded. "How are you calling me from a regular phone number and not from the prison wall phone?"

"Never mind that," Freddy whispered and peeped around the cutoff corner to make sure he was still alone. "You busy in a couple days?" Freddy asked.

"No, not really. What's up?"

"I'm planning an escape."

"Are you serious? It's about fucking time, dude! You just let me know what I need to do. Oh yeah, and my boyfriend just recently stole a car too. It might make a good getaway vehicle. He was going to take it to the chop shop, but I'll talk him out of it," Star cheerfully said.

Freddy gave her the plan.

"Sounds like a plan, Freddy. Let me know if anything changes."

"Sounds good. Talk to you soon." Freddy hung up and went back to his room, so he could get some rest.

"This is going to be interesting," Freddy whispered to himself.

CHAPTER 8

After a good night's rest, Freddy was awakened by the daily cancelation announcements. It was just a part of the daily routine.

Freddy had a little less than thirty minutes before they call for the chapel goers to go to service, so he got up and got ready. Freddy got up a little too quickly and felt the excruciating pain on his lower stomach from the fresh tattoo. It still felt raw. Freddy aided his fresh ink, applying a triple antibiotic cream to it, so he could move around freely. Freddy knew his time here at the prison was short, and there was no room for failure, so everything Freddy needed to do today he needed to execute perfectly and accordingly. This shift was a good shift for him to make this getaway because the officers were short-staffed, and the yard usually ran itself.

Once the announcements for the chapel were made, Freddy grabbed a brand-new Bible and headed for the door when he was stopped by a crazy-looking inmate with a lazy eye. He kind of looked like a lizard to an extent with the bone structure in his face.

"Yo, Freddy, look here. I got these two Seroquels four hundred milligrams. They are the strongest ones you can get. I am trying to sell them."

"And what price are you asking for?" Freddy replied.

"I'm not going to be picky. I'm sure you can think of something," the lizard said shyly.

Fucking faggot, Freddy thought. "Oh, yeah, sure. Give me the pills. I gotta go," Freddy said and held out his hand.

"Here you go." The pills were given to Freddy. "But I have to warn you, a whole pill is too strong for you. I would recommend only taking fifty milligrams at a time. That's enough to make you sleep for two days. That way one pill will last you over a week. And I gave you two!"

"Thanks. Now get out of my way," Freddy demanded as he put the pills in his pocket.

"Don't forget to pay me!" the lizard yelled out the door, but Freddy was already walking through the gate.

*****

The chapel was packed. There was even a line of inmates outside the chapel waiting to get inside. It would be difficult to locate Eggshell because Freddy did not know what he looked like. The only thing Freddy knew is that he was a chapel worker, so he was in here somewhere. Also, it would not be a good idea to ask around for him because it might blow his cover. Freddy did not want that to happen, so he will just make it inside first and maybe attend the church service to make his intentions look pure and angelic.

Once inside, Freddy observed his surroundings, noticing that there were not any inmates that may resemble a chapel worker just standing around anywhere. They were all hoarding to the service. Once Freddy made it into the service room, he tried looking for a seat, but it was difficult. The room was slam packed. Freddy saw a few open seats here and there, but he did not want to sit near a bunch of people he did not know. He continued walking down the aisle and bingo! He found the perfect seat on the front row, almost right in front of the preacher's stage. Freddy sat and waited for the rest of the inmates to flood the service. The last inmate took his seat, and an officer shut the big double doors that everyone walked through. The shutting of the doors was so loud that everyone turned their heads. Freddy noticed that there was a single inmate standing in the back of the service room with his back to the wall near the doors.

That had to be Eggshell. See how fast Freddy figured that out? Before Freddy could get up, the preacher made an announcement.

"Hello, everybody! What an amazing day this is going to be. All I ask of you all is to please remain seated during our service."

"Fucking Christ," Freddy let out kind of loudly and everybody, including the preacher, turned their heads in disgust toward Freddy.

The preacher continued anyway.

About five minutes into the service, Freddy pulled his dick out of his pants and started jacking off, holding his open Bible over his dick with his other hand.

After a couple of minutes, the preacher caught Freddy in the act and acted frantically.

"Someone stop him! He's…he's…he's jacking!" the preacher man yelled and pointed out Freddy.

"No, I'm not! Tell the truth!" Freddy yelled back as he covered himself back up again.

The officer made it down the aisle and motioned for Freddy to exit the chapel, or there would be some serious consequences. Freddy obeyed, and the officer watched from the front row Freddy exiting the service room. As Freddy was pushing the double doors open, he stopped and got the inmate standing next to the door's attention.

"Eggshell?"

The man did not respond. Instead he looked a little bit agitated and motioned Freddy to leave with his hands. Freddy pushed onto the doors and was now back in the lobby area where he had just waited to get in. Before Freddy was able to leave the chapel, the man standing by the door swooped into the lobby and got Freddy's attention.

"Let me ask you a question, son. Why are you looking for Eggshell?" he asked.

"So you are Eggshell?"

"You didn't answer the question. Why are you—"

The man was cut off.

"I'm here to transport a package," Freddy stated.

"Okay, I was just making sure. I'm not Eggshell by the way."

"Then who the fuck are you, and why did you just get into my business?" Freddy was getting mad now.

"I'm Eggyolk. Come on, Eggshell is in the chaplain's office arranging the religious books."

Freddy felt dumbfounded and in wonder how certain inmates get their nicknames.

Freddy had to ask, "How did you guys get those names?"

"It's a long story. You really don't want to know."

Eggyolk led Freddy to the chap's office, where Eggshell sat in a very comfy-looking chair next to a very neat and organized bookshelf. The aroma of coffee flooded the room. It was almost overwhelming, and Freddy had to take a breath before entering.

"Ah, so you're the one that Tweak sent," Eggshell exclaimed as he stood up and shook Freddy's hand.

"You don't know where his hand has been recently, Shell," Eggyolk warned.

"Listen to your friend," Freddy added.

Eggshell wiped his hand on his pants and then turned around and lifted the cushion on the fancy chair and revealed a big package of contraband wrapped tightly up in plastic wrap.

"How the hell am I suppo—"

Freddy was cut off by Shell. "Easy. Just put on this jacket and hold the bomb under your arm. Inside of the jacket of course."

"All right and one more thing," Freddy stated. "Do you have something for me for transporting this?"

"Yes, I do actually." Shell reached for a book on the bookshelf and opened it to where his bookmark was and took the bookmark and tried to hand it to Freddy. It was small and very skinny. It looked like it was torn off a piece of paper.

"You have to be kidding me," Freddy said.

"Calm down, Freddy. This is K2 or deuce. Whatever you want to call it. The chemicals were sprayed onto this paper. It's easier to get it inside of the prison that way," Eggshell said. "But I have to warn you, this shit is far more potent than the average K2 that everyone smokes. Take one hit and put the blunt out. You will go on a wild ride."

"All right," Freddy said and stuck the K2 in his pocket with the two pills he forgot he had.

"Fucking Christ," Freddy said.

"Oh, and one more thing before you leave." Shell produced another book from the shelf and handed it to Freddy. "Freddy, that's a *Dungeons and Dragons* player's book. There are a lot of new powers and abilities in it. If anyone tries to stop you, tell them I gave you that."

"Smart thinking, Shell," Eggyolk said and escorted Freddy to the chapel exit.

"I'll see you guys again soon," Freddy lied.

As soon as Freddy left the chapel, he saw the head contraband officer walking down the sidewalk heading straight for Freddy.

Shit. Those bitches just set me up, Freddy thought.

If there was one thing any inmate had to worry about, it was the contraband officers. They were the assholes that are known for strip searching inmates and kicking in their doors, taking anything they felt you couldn't have and charging you for it.

"Dawson, where do you think you're going? Service isn't over yet. Go back in, so I can do a routine search on you," contraband said.

Freddy's heart just dropped. He knew he could take a little drug charge for the pills and the K2, but he had no idea what was in the package underneath his arm. Probably meth, heroin, weed, tattoo ink, and paraphernalia items. He could get street charges, resulting him getting more time added to his sentence and possibly have to do federal time.

Contraband spoke again, "Woah, what's that in your hand?" He took the book from Freddy and examined it. "*D and D*, huh? Is this what you're into? I'll have you know that I am a magician with an invisible cloak. I could be a good addition to your team."

Freddy played along and tried to sound nerdy, "I am currently a warlock. And I have the ability to stun my foes, so I can move twice in one turn. I'm trying to evolve into a mage. And in my other game, I am an avion, and I can fly over everything."

"Are you going to continue playing when you get out of prison?" contraband said.

"Absolutely. I'll be going to competitions and conventions any time I can go. My whole life is absorbed by this game. I love it."

"All right, Dawson. Go ahead back to your dorm. I'll shake you down later."

Without question, Freddy marched down the sidewalk, almost speed walking. Without a doubt, he looked like he was guilty and up to no good.

*****

Once Freddy made it back to the dorm, he went straight to Tweak's room. He was not there. Freddy was about to have a heart attack.

"Fucking Christ, where is he?"

Freddy turned back around and saw Tweak making his way up the hall.

"Yo, Freddy, I had this crazy dream last night that you tried to escape this bitch, but you got caught! That shit was crazy," Tweak said loudly as he was coming down the corridor to his room.

Things were getting strange now. For some reason, to Freddy, junkies have special powers similar to dogs having a sixth sense to sense danger brewing up. When it came to things such as criminal activities or even an accident causing serious injury or even death, it was the junkies who walked away scotch free with nothing over his or her head. It's like they are untouchable. With all of these mysterious events going on, first with the contraband man, now with Tweak's dream. All of this is triggering Freddy to become paranoid schizophrenic, and now he is beginning to question prior events like getting his tattoo, getting a cell phone, fucking Clardy, and things of that nature. Hopefully it's just his mind playing tricks on himself.

"Freddy?" Tweak asked.

Freddy snapped back into reality. "Oh my bad, I thought I heard something. But yeah, that's a crazy dream you had. I wouldn't do that though. I had a crazy dream last night too. I fucked Jesus Christ on the *Stonehenge*."

"Damn, that's smack nasty, dude!"

Freddy's paranoia kicked back in, "Wh-what did you say?"

"Smack nasty. Like the tattoo that I just did on you?"

Freddy was losing his marbles, but he tried extra hard to bounce back to reality this time. "I got your package and really want to know what's in it. Can we open it?"

"We can. Technically I'm not supposed to because this package is not mine. It's for someone else in here that I owe. Hey, is that a *Dungeons and Dragons* book?" Tweak asked.

"Wait a second. This bomb isn't yours? What the fuck is going on right now?"

"Freddy, just chill. Let's open the pack up, be nosy for a bit, and wrap it back up the way that it was. Then we'll take it to him."

"*We?*" Freddy yelled.

"Yes, *we*. I think he might want to buy your book from you."

They began unwrapping the package, only to find colorful stones, dust, various forms of jewels, tarot cards, lemon juice, holy water, fancy-looking leaves, and other miscellaneous things like a lighter and a spell book, along with some unidentified items.

Freddy got serious. "Tweak, who is this package for?"

"The Wiccan. Nobody knows his name. We just call him the Wiccan. You know anything about Wicca, you know, the devil worshippers?"

"No, and I'm not sure if I want to," Freddy stated.

"Well, lucky for you, he's not here yet, but once he gets back to the dorm, I'm coming to get you so we can pull up on him."

"Fucking Christ. Fine," Freddy said and headed back to his room.

Tweak yelled down the aisle as Freddy was leaving, "Oh and one more thing! The Wiccan's roommate molested a child. Just giving you a heads-up!"

Freddy thought about that soda that he deeboed.

"Wonderful," he said back.

This whole time Freddy was sweating bullets because he thought there was a bunch of drugs in that package. It was almost a relief that it wasn't, but he still felt like a complete idiot.

CHAPTER 9

It had been a long morning already, and there was plenty enough time remaining in the day. Freddy's escape will be happening tomorrow, and he did not plan on rescheduling it. In the meantime, Freddy felt as if him and Kim developed a good, trustworthy relationship as roommates now, so Freddy believed through the power of manipulation that he can ask Kim more personal questions about him. Hopefully Kim was buttered up enough.

Freddy broke the silence between them in the room. "Hey, Kim, I'm supposed to be getting a few Kool-Aid packs later on tonight for us."

"Really? I didn't even know they sold them."

"They don't," Freddy replied. "I just know the right people on the yard."

"You know some good people then," Kim stated.

"I do. In fact, you're one of them. You have been one of my best roommates. I can tell at heart that you're a good dude, and it's a blessing that both of us are maxing out soon," Freddy said.

Kim jumped back, "Who are you telling? I'm lucky I didn't get fed time, and this is my second offense! I hope my father doesn't try to—"

Freddy cut him off, "Your father? I meant to ask you the other day what your charges were, but I didn't want you to think I was trying to get in your business or anything like that."

"You're good, Freddy," Kim chimed. "I trust you. You've showed me a lot back here, and I can call you my friend. I'm back here because, well, my father...my father made some mistakes.

Freddy looked intrigued and listened as Kim fell into his own trap.

"You see, my father is a very, very powerful man. I believe he has strings with the triad and the Yakuza, though he will not say so himself. He knows presidents of certain Asian countries, and he can always ask them for help."

Freddy interrupted, "Well, what kind of work does he do?"

"That's the thing. All of his work is underground and illegal. He tries to include me in some fashion with his work. He does fraud, racketeering, extortion, kidnapping, murder. Anything involving drugs, you name it. How I got caught up was by the works of him, but I am fine with that because I don't ever have anything to worry about when I get home. I live in luxury, eat good. Anytime I need something, I can get it. We never have to stress economically, and it's all because of my father."

"What's his name?" Freddy asked, hoping Kim would not get suspicious.

"His name is Ho Chen Xu."

Freddy was confused. "I thought your name was Ho Chen Xu."

"It is," Kim replied.

"So you're a junior?"

"No, just Ho Chen Xu."

Freddy was very boggled by Kim's story. "Kim, please explain—"

Kim cut him off, "You see, when I was born, my father instructed my mother not to reveal who the father of me was. She acted like she did not know who the father was. Therefore, I am not my father's junior. My mother even kept her pregnancy a secret."

"So how did all of this get you in trouble, Kim?"

"I'm about to tell you," Kim snapped. "My father and I have the same name. Everything my father buys, he puts it in my name, so his name is clean. It is very, very rare that our family has any run-ins with the law. My father is very organized and takes precautions for anything. I am instructed that if I get into trouble with the law, I take responsibility and keep my mouth shut, and I will continue to live in luxury. I am also not permitted to give SCDC any emergency contacts. All of my ties with my father are to be kept a secret so my father can continue his work."

Freddy remained speechless as Kim's story unfolded. This is a sad, sad life story. For the rest of Kim's life, he will just be his father's lackey and scapegoat. Freddy can almost foresee Kim spending his life in prison because of his dad. It will be a never-ending cycle, and Kim is just completely oblivious to the bigger picture that he is just being used. Freddy kind of likes it.

"Wow, Kim. That's a crazy story. You are very lucky you live in luxury and don't have to work," Freddy stated. "Look, I have a proposition for you. I really need some good work when I get out, and I have nowhere to turn. Do you think maybe you could refer me to your father? You already know I'm not a crash dummy, and I know how to move," Freddy asked eagerly, hoping his manipulation has worked.

Kim's voice softened a bit, "I know you would be a good addition to my dad's aide, but unfortunately I cannot contact him back here. But what I can do is give you an address and a phone number, and all you have to say is that I sent you. The rest is up to you," Kim said as he started writing down the information on a little scrap piece of paper and then produced it to Freddy.

"Perfect, bro. Thank you. Maybe soon I can live a luxury life."

Freddy's post-prison life was truly revealing itself. The thought of all these things was sending shivers down Freddy's spine. Everything was falling into place. You never know who you're going to meet in prison. That doesn't matter because Freddy was still going to teach Kim a lesson despite of Kim's openness and generosity. But before he did that, he now waited for Tweak so that they can handle business with the Wiccan.

Out of curiosity, Freddy picked up the *Dungeons and Dragons* book and studied it to pass the time.

CHAPTER 10

It was now nine twenty at night, and Freddy and Kim were just getting comfortable when Tweak ran into the room.

"What the hell are you waiting for? Let's go, Freddy, he's waiting on us!" Tweak said frantically.

"All right, all right. Just don't have a stroke." Freddy grabbed the book, and they began walking to the Wiccan's room.

Halfway there, the lizard man appeared and bumped into Freddy.

"Oh, hey, Freddy. I was just coming to see you. I hope you can pay me off tonight," the lizard said.

"Oh yeah, you know it. I will pay you off very well tonight, my friend," he replied. "Hold up for a bit though and let me finish some business."

The lizard walked off and Freddy looked at Tweak.

"Don't ask."

"I was not going to," Tweak replied.

"Good. Now stay here. I'll be right back." Freddy turned around and ran back to his room and confronted Kim.

"Yo, Kim, I got those Kool-Aid packs. Make sure you don't fall asleep. I'll be back in a few."

Kim nodded and Freddy ran back to where he left Tweak, who seemed annoyed. They followed each other to the Wiccan's room, where he had his whole package sprawled out on his bunk, all separated accordingly. His child molester roommate just laid there with the Bible open on the table next to his as if he just got done reading it.

The Wiccan, looking very serious and very creepy, welcomed them into the room.

"Are you Freddy?" the Wiccan asked with a monotone and boring voice.

Freddy nodded.

"Ah, yes. Thank you for getting all of my things for me. I needed it. May I look at your book?"

Freddy handed him the book and spoke, "What is all of that anyway? Pixie dust?"

The Wiccan looked up and gave Freddy a death stare. "I take what I do very seriously. Wicca is not for everybody. It might not be for you."

"Well, isn't Wicca witchcraft?" Freddy asked and quickly glanced back just to see that Tweak had disappeared, leaving Freddy and the two roommates alone.

"Fuck," he whispered to himself. "But yeah, Mr. Wiccan, isn't it just a bunch of devil worshipping and witchcraft?"

The Wiccan finally let out a small chuckle. "Please call me Scotty, and my roommate's name is Earl."

Freddy was not concerned about Earl at all, but before Scotty was able to respond to Freddy's question, Freddy noticed that Earl was holding up his Bible and was trying to motion warn Freddy not to ask Scotty any more questions.

Freddy snapped and exposed Earl, "Don't give me that shit, Earl! All of you child rapists are the fucking same. You sick bastards mess up in the outside world and then all of a sudden want to turn to Jesus and Christianity when you get locked up." All of this was giving Freddy flashbacks from when he was a kid. Freddy continued, "And I'll have you know something. I will never be anything like you or your friends. All of that Holy Bible, God, Jesus, yada yada nonsense, you can leave me out of it. I'm not with it, and I am trying to learn something. So please continue, Scotty."

The room got quiet for a second.

"Right." Scotty cleared his throat and turned around for a quick second just to give Earl a hard stare for trying to intrude. "I understand your question, Freddy, but here is the truth. Yes, there is witchcraft but let me explain something. Wicca is a religion. Witchcraft is just witchcraft. You can use it if you choose to, though I do not recommend it. And frankly you don't have to be a Wiccan to use witchcraft. You can be Islamic, Christian, Buddhist, or hell, you don't need to be religious to use it, and that is what the world fails to understand. The practices of Wicca is not meant for harm, but it's not meant to be played with either. And about that devil worship remark you made, that's a joke in my eyes."

"I see," Freddy responded. "So what are Wicca's beliefs?"

"What are your beliefs?" Scotty asked.

Freddy really did not know, so he remained silent.

"That's right, I'm not obligating you to tell me," Scotty said. "That is why I enjoy Wicca. You believe what you want to believe. Just don't force it on anyone else. Basically, you are painting your own world's portrait. Wicca is a complete nature-based religion, and there are lots of practices involving plants, herbs, elements, and things of that nature."

Freddy is very intrigued.

"A lot of people do not realize this, but a lot of today's medicines derive from plants. So the people are taking these medications to heal themselves from whatever is hurting them. But little do they know that those medications are a practice of Wicca. Even the makers probably don't think twice about it. Energy is a huge factor as well. Here in prison, the energy is very negative, and it is very contagious. But I'll get into that another time."

Freddy finally spoke, "I have made my decision now. I am a Wiccan. Everything you have told me makes complete sense, and I am fascinated."

Freddy looked on Scotty's bunk and saw a Ouija board. He had seen them being used on old movies, but he had never played with one himself.

"Can we use that Ouija board? I want to contact my father and ask a couple things."

Scotty lowered his head and finally spoke, "Usually I would say no because this board needs to be operated by someone with a lot of experience, but given you helped me out with my package, I will make an exception for this special occasion."

Scotty set up a small table in the middle of the room and placed the board on it. He then reached for a few things that came out of his package.

"Please enlighten me what you are doing with that stuff," Freddy stated.

"Of course. I will start off by burning some sage." Scotty then placed a small-looking crystal near the board. "This is fluorite. Fluorite helps with your meditation, dreams, and draws out negativity, similar to the sage that I am now burning. Next is the herb frankincense. It will give you the spiritual visions, astral strength, and protection. The only issue with the frankincense is that it gets its energy from the sun. And since it is dark, I'll just shine my lamp over it while it's burning. I know it looks unprofessional, but it'll just have to do," Scotty stated.

"Now what?" Freddy asked.

"I want you to go into a meditative state. Visualize your dad. Feel his energy as if he is in this room with us. Do this for a minute."

Once everything was burning, Freddy did what he was told. With that being done, Freddy nodded, indicating that he is ready, and they both put their fingers on the oculus indicator. Scotty led by moving the indicator three times in a clockwise circle and started the conversation.

"Hello, is anyone present with Freddy and I?" Scotty said into the air.

It took a couple seconds, but the indicator jolted, startling both Freddy and Scotty, forcing its way to the "yes" corner of the board.

Scotty spoke again, "I apologize if we angered you, but my partner has a couple of questions."

The spirit lightened up its pull a little bit, moved the indicator around, and went back to "yes."

Freddy spoke, "Dad, is that you?"

This time, his dad's spirit spelled it out Y-E-S.

"I have always wondered…who was the cause of your death?"

Y-O-U-R M-O-M.

"I had my suspicions. She has issues."

P-I-L-L-S A-L-C-O-H-O-L.

"I have one more question. Is what I'm planning to do tomorrow a good idea?"

Y-E-S Y-E-S Y-E-S Y-E-S Y-E-S.

His dad's spirit would not stop saying yes until Freddy spoke once again, "Thank you, Dad. Goodbye."

Freddy's dad spelled out I-L-Y and then the indictor moved to the goodbye section of the board.

Scotty and Freddy took their hands off of the oculus indicator.

"Success!" Scotty exclaimed. "Is there anything else you want done before I get some shut-eye?"

"Yes, I would like to cast one spell on myself. I need protection and luck."

"Very well. I'll tell you that the best thing you need for those two is a tiger's eye, but given our circumstances and our location in America, that will not work. So I will have to use what I have which will be fern and figwort."

Freddy tried not to laugh.

After the spell, Freddy was satisfied.

"Just one more thing before I go, Scotty. I'm about to crush up these two Seroquel pills, and I need a piece of paper to put the powder in and don't ask."

Scotty produced the paper, and Freddy took the pills out of his pocket and crushed them up with a can of chili beans and put the powder on the paper and folded the paper numerous times and stuck it back in his pocket.

Scotty chimed in, sounding just like the *Marvel* superhero *Thor*, "May the gods bless you with the Ur rune. It is the release of creative power that proceeds a new cycle of activity. It is helpful. Therefore where there is space for new ideas, a fresh start, a change of circumstances, an immediate boost in morale, it challenges you to have the courage to let go of things you no longer need, then you will allow new possibilities to arise. Oh, and good luck on your escape tomorrow."

Freddy freaked out, "How did you—"

"I think even a dummy could read between the lines. Plus, I casted a flax spell on myself earlier, and I made sure I only used the seeds this time. Enhances psychic powers and healing. Have a nice life." Scotty smiled.

"Thank you for everything. Maybe I will see you again some time," Freddy said, nodded his head, and left the room.

The night had just begun.

CHAPTER 11

"Hey Kim," Freddy said as he just popped back into the room. "Hand me my drinking bottle on the table please. And hand me yours too. I'm going to fill them up with cold water."

Kim did so.

Before Freddy stopped at the water fountain, he approached the lizard man, who was standing by himself by the bookshelf that never had any books on it.

"In exactly one hour, meet me in the first shower. You'll see that I pay my bills," Freddy said proudly.

"Okay, I will be there."

Freddy proceeded to fill the bottles up. He took the Seroquel powder out of his pocket and dumped all of the powder into Kim's bottle, secured the lid, and shook it up. The water still was clear and pristine. You could not even tell it was contaminated.

He then stopped by Scotty and Earl's room one final time. Scotty was asleep, but Earl was still wide awake with earbuds in his ears. He pulled them out when he saw Freddy.

"Yo, Earl. One last thing. Do you know who wrote the Holy Bible? It was Shakespeare. That's right, it was William Shakespeare," Freddy said in a stern, sarcastic manner then went into Earl's locker and took two fruit punch drink mix packets for himself. "See you in hell, brother."

Freddy went back to his room, set Kim's bottle next to Kim along with the drink packet. Kim instantly untwisted the cap and poured the contents of the packet into the water and shook it up. He opened it up and smelled it.

"Mmm. Fruit punch, my favorite," Kim admitted and chugged the entire bottle.

"Damn," Freddy said. "Pretty thirsty, huh?"

"I was. I waited a long time for that Kool-Aid. It tastes a little weird though, but it's probably because I haven't had any in a long time."

"Yeah, that's probably what it was." Freddy smiled.

Kim stood up. "Freddy, I have to say. You are a very cool dude, and I fuck with you the long ways. My father will be happy to have you on the team." Kim then gave Freddy a fist bump.

Freddy laughed. "I appreciate it, bro, but I'm going to teach you a valuable lesson. The ones that you fuck with the most, you have to watch the most. Not saying I'm pointing fingers at myself or anything. Just giving you some insight."

"I understand, that's good advice."

With the conversation now over, Freddy waited for the pills to kick in.

Twenty-five minutes later, Kim was knocked out. Freddy tried to wake him up, but Kim was so out of it that he could not fight the effects of the pills and could only mumble unintelligent things.

Perfect.

Freddy did the hard part first by getting Kim out of his clothes and into the skirt and crop top, the same ones Freddy wore himself when he got his last victim, Foot. Freddy then did his makeup. And he went heavy on it. Satisfied and with about ten minutes to spare, Freddy began jacking off to his creation.

It did not take him long. Freddy came into a rag and began wiping all of the walls in his room with it, including both lockers. There was nothing wrong with leaving your mark before you left.

Freddy raised Kim up off the bed and stood him up.

Freddy kept his arm around his shoulders, so he would not stumble and then whispered in his ear, "Ho Chen Xu. Or should I do the honor of changing your name? Sum Dum Ho has a nice ring. I'm going with that."

Freddy walked Sum Dum Ho all the way to the first shower, where the lizard was already waiting.

"He's yours for the rest of the night," Freddy said, exhausted from the long haul.

Freddy then went to bed.

*****

Freddy was awakened two hours later, hearing a bunch of commotion coming from near the front door and the main area and quickly jumped out to investigate. There were numerous officers standing around the bathroom.

"Fucking Christ," Freddy whispered, moving in a little bit closer.

He overheard a nurse from inside the bathroom. "He is deceased. I checked his pulse, and he does not have one," she said.

Sum Dum Ho had been fucked to death.

Moments later, they took Kim out on the stretcher. Following him was the lizard man in handcuffs being escorted by a few officers.

"It was consensual, I swear! Why I am in handcuffs?" he was yelling as he was shown out of the building.

Freddy had a feeling that he was next, but he had time. He knew this prison was so sorry that they would not investigate this until the next shift comes. This means Freddy had to escape sooner than expected.

Freddy got on his cell phone in his room and called Starlene.

"Freddy? It's like two something in the morning. What's up?" a tired Star said.

"Listen. We're on for tomorrow. Be in the parking lot at seven thirty. That is in six hours. I have a good plan," Freddy said quietly.

"Okay, my boyfriend has a stolen car. Me and him will be there. Love you." She hung up.

Freddy just knew that the lizard was going to snitch on him now.

CHAPTER 12

Freddy woke up early. He wanted to make his final preparations for his smack-nasty escape. Freddy still had that strip of K2, and this would be a detrimental factor and play a big role if everything goes according to plan. He had been paying attention to all of the shift's officers, and he had assumed that this was the best shift for him. He grabbed his K2 and left the room.

He was on the look for the biggest Black guy in the dorm who happened to be one of the biggest deuce heads on the yard as well. This man's name was Boston. It wasn't too hard to find him. As soon as Freddy walked into the main area, Boston was using the microwave. He was by himself, so Freddy approached him.

"Hey, Boston. I have something for you."

"And what might that be?" Boston asked as he looked confused.

His confusion was normal and expected because him and Freddy have never spoke a word to each other before. Freddy pulled the strip of K2 out of his pocket and handed it to him.

"What's this for?" Boston asked.

Freddy remembered the warning about this strip's potency. "Someone gave me a couple strips yesterday. I smoked the other one last night. It wasn't that strong. You have to smoke the whole blunt just to get a buzz," Freddy lied, big time.

"Word? Appreciate that, dude. I'm going to smoke it right before I go to work," Boston said.

This was perfect because they go to work around the seven-fifteen mark. It was six forty.

With just a few minutes to spare, Freddy went to the dayroom. He saw Scotty on the back row, drinking a cup of coffee. Freddy joined him as he waited to see Boston head into the bathroom with his blunt. But that should be in a few minutes, so Freddy started the conversation.

"Ah, Scotty. I thought about it, right, I'm going to tell you my beliefs."

"I'm all ears."

"I believe this life we are living is just a simulation. When you die, that ends the simulation, and the longer you live in it, the more credits you earn for your next simulation. Of course, you'll get credits for your good deeds and gestures as well. My next simulation is going to be awful because I am a horrible person, so all of my credits will come from a long life."

"Very interesting, Freddy. So you lose credits when you do bad things?"

"Absolutely."

"So what you're saying is if I had a perfect simulation and did extraordinary things in it, that my next life, or simulation, would be based on how well I did in my previous one."

"That is correct." Freddy smiled. "But don't get it twisted. Your next may be fascinating and awesome but mess your credits up in it and the following simulation after that will be a lot worse. And anything could happen. You might die in your teens."

Scotty beamed in closer. "You are a very intelligent person, and this is an awesome theory. But don't force it on the next person."

"I don't plan to. I don't think about it. People think I'm crazy already. Oh shit! I'll be right back."

Freddy forgot his knife in his room, and he needed the knife for the escape. Freddy ran back to the room, grabbed the knife that he magnetted to the bottom of his locker, lodged it into his pants for easy access, and went back to the main area.

As soon as he stepped in, he saw Boston speed walking to the bathroom with his shower things. Who showers before they go to work in the PI? It doesn't make much sense because the plant is a dirty job, but Freddy doesn't really give a fuck.

It's showtime.

Freddy waited patiently for a minute or two over by the microwave when he finally heard a big thud from inside the bathroom. After a few courtesy seconds, Freddy finally proceeded toward the bathroom so that he could see what had happened, but he had to fight through the flock of the other nosy inmates that beat him to it. Sure enough, Boston was laid out on the shower floor, butt naked. Two inmates tried to help Boston up, but his deadweight made him collapse to the ground again. Except this time, when he hit the ground, he began masturbating uncontrollably. The inmates in the background went crazy and cheered Boston on. The two inmates who tried to help him up just completely stopped what they were doing and looked at each other.

"Call me a snitch if you want, I don't give a fuck. I'm getting the police," one of them finally said.

Boston rolled around in a fetal position, now aiming himself toward the inmates, jacking even more violently than before.

"Oh my god," Freddy mumbled.

Shit was about to get serious. Freddy fell back, so he could observe everything, so he could be ready to make his move. The officer finally came and pushed his way through the crowd and just stood in the doorway of the bathroom.

"You have to be kidding me," he said.

The officer let out a huge sigh and hit the button on his radio.

"Operations thirty-six. I need the entire *A* team first responders up here immediately. No, nobody is hurt yet. We are going to need the stretcher. He's-he's…jacking. Like crazy. No, he does not have any clothes on, and I don't know where his clothes even are. It's as if he went to the bathroom butt naked."

Freddy peeped out the front door and saw the entire team consisting of regular officers, lieutenants, the captain, the major, and some people he didn't even know heading straight for the dorm. But one person stood out to Freddy, and he was in the very back. Lt. Hickenbottom.

Freddy went outside and hid in the security closet just a few feet from the front door, unnoticed. The gates popped and Freddy waited for his man. The other *A* team members stormed right past Freddy.

He heard Hickenbottom's nerdy voice as he closed the gates shut behind him and moved in closer. As soon as Hickenbottom got to the closet, Freddy surprised him and snatched him into the closet. Freddy beat him until he was unconscious.

Now it was time to switch clothes.

As the LT was stripped of his uniform, Freddy took out his knife and cut Hickenbottom's dick off. It was of high resemblance to a Vienna sausage.

"This will be a nice gift for the trainee at the gatehouse," Freddy said to him as he began putting on the officer uniform and vest.

Once done, Freddy exited the closet, leaving Hickenbottom in it. Freddy approached the gate and hit the button on the radio and tried to sound like Hickenbottom.

"Ninety-three, thirty-six. This is Lt. Hickenbottom. Pop gates one and two."

The gates popped and Freddy entered the sally port, shutting both gates behind him. Freddy walked to the gatehouse, and luckily, it was unlocked.

"I need to get a fresh can of Mace out of my car and my face shield," Freddy said to the confused trainee who absolutely had no idea what she had just done, "but I have a surprise for you." Freddy placed the penis on the table in front of her.

She gasped.

"I'll be right back."

Freddy opened the front door of the gatehouse and stepped into the parking lot. As if on cue, a purple Kia Soul pulled into the lot. Star and her boyfriend were inside it. Freddy ran up to it.

"Really? Your stolen cat is a purple Kia Soul? You've got to be fucking kidding me."

"Shut up and get in. There's a change of clothes for you in the back seat," Star snapped.

Freddy did so and they pulled off.

As they were leaving, they saw Boston being carried on the stretcher to the gates. He was still jacking.

"Oh my god, is he really doing that?" Star asked.

Freddy rolled down the window and heard all of the inmates hollering and cheering still.

"It's been a crazy morning," Freddy replied.

*****

About a mile up the road, the trio pulled behind an old, abandoned business on the side of the road.

"My car is here," Star said. "We need to ditch this retarded Soul."

"I agree," her boyfriend, Tom, said.

They did so and Freddy got in the back seat, leaving the officer uniform in the Soul. The first thing Freddy noticed was the Taurus .357 revolver underneath the driver's seat. Freddy knew what it was for.

They drove off.

*****

After being on the road for an hour and a half, Star spoke out, "About a mile up the road from here, there's a dirt road that leads to a big field. I want to smoke a blunt. You guys cool with that?"

"Absolutely," Tom replied.

Freddy just remained silent.

"I love you, Tom," Star said shyly.

"Love you too, baby doll."

"How cute," Freddy said.

As they got to the dirt road, Star made the turn, and they soon reached the field. She put the car in park, and they just sat there.

"You know the rules, boys. No smoking in the car."

They all got out of the car, and Star lit the blunt. They passed it back and forth and carried on conversations. Once the whole blunt had been smoked, it was time to hit the road again.

"Hold up," Tom said. "I have to take a mean piss. I've been holding it all morning."

Tom stepped about thirty feet away and began peeing. Star smiled and looked at Freddy. Nothing was said. Freddy raised up the .357 and aimed it at Tom. Star covered her ears. Freddy pulled the trigger, and the back of Tom's head exploded.

"I was wondering when you were going to do that," Star said and gave Freddy a big hug. She then got on her knees and began giving her twin brother, Freddy, a blowjob.

Once they were done, Star looked up at Freddy. "Where to now?" she asked.

Freddy reached into his pocket and pulled out the address that Kim gave him. He looked at it.

"Next stop, Columbia."

ABOUT THE AUTHOR

The less you know about the author, the better.